For my little Jérôme and
for the great Jirô Taniguchi — N.R.

This edition published by Kids Can Press in 2016

Originally published in French under the title
Le grand livre des petits trésors by Comme des géants inc.

Text © 2015 Nadine Robert
Illustrations © 2015 Aki

Translation rights arranged through VeroK Agency, Spain
English translation © 2016 Kids Can Press
English translation by Yvette Ghione

Kids Can Press acknowledges the financial support of the Government
of Ontario, through the Ontario Media Development Corporation's
Ontario Book Initiative; the Ontario Arts Council; the Canada Council
for the Arts; and the Government of Canada, through the CBF, for our
publishing activity.

Published in Canada by
Kids Can Press Ltd.
25 Dockside Drive
Toronto, ON M5A 0B5

Published in the U.S. by
Kids Can Press Ltd.
2250 Military Road
Tonawanda, NY 14150

www.kidscanpress.com

The text is set in Remo Pro.

Original edition edited by Nadine Robert and Mathieu Lavoie
English edition edited by Yvette Ghione
Designed by Mathieu Lavoie

Manufactured in Shenzhen, China, in 10/2015, by C & C Offset.

CM 16 0 9 8 7 6 5 4 3 2 1

Library and Archives Canada Cataloguing in Publication

Robert, Nadine, 1971–
[Grand livre des petits trésors. English]
Toshi's little treasures / written by Nadine Robert ; illustrated by Aki.

Translation of: Le grand livre des petits trésors.
English translation by Yvette Ghione.
ISBN 978-1-77138-573-2 (bound)

    1. Natural history — Juvenile literature. 2. Nature — Juvenile
literature. I. Aki, 1987–, illustrator II. Ghione, Yvette, translator III. Title.
IV. Title: Grand livre des petits trésors. English.

QH48.R6213 2015   j508   C2015-904629-7

Kids Can Press is a corus™ Entertainment company

Nadine Robert · Aki

Toshi's Little Treasures

Kids Can Press

There you are,
Toshi!

Hi,
Grandma!

Look what
I have for you.

Oh!

A nice new
backpack to carry
all the little things you
collect on our walks.

For my
treasures!

Exactly.
Let's go!

I thought we could take a walk along the river this morning.

branch

chain link

pebbles

I found a see-through leaf!

Hmm. I think it's an insect wing.

bottle cap

piece of glass

dish shard

mussels

claw

shell

cattails

lure

reed
tufts

Little Riverside Treasures

an old
bottle cap

a crayfish
claw

a ceramic dish
shard

a fishing lure
without a hook

a dragonfly
wing

an old
chain link

an empty
snail shell

a cattail

a pussy willow
branch

reed tufts

a piece of
polished glass

a perfectly smooth
skipping stone

Each treasure is connected to something on this page. Can you find their matches?

1

2

3

4

5

6

7

8

9

10

11

12

You'll find the answers at the end of the book.

matchbox

bead

nutshells

whistle

sunglasses lens

Little City Treasures

a necklace bead

a marble

a dog whistle

a guitar pick

a hair barrette

a nutshell

a gingko leaf

an old
square head nail

an empty
matchbox

decorative
stones

magnolia blossom
petals

a sunglasses
lens

Can you find a match for each of Toshi's treasures?

1

2

3

4

5

6

7

8

9

10

11

12

Check the answers at the back of the book.

Today we're going for a walk in the forest!

acorn

rock

holly berries

chestnut

fern shoots

maple key

snake skin

Little Forest Treasures

a partridge
feather

a soda can
tab

a chestnut
and its casing

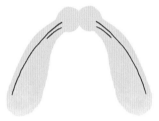

a double
maple key

holly berries

lilies of the valley
flowers

a pinecone

a fern shoot

shed snake skin

a goldfinch
egg

an acorn

a rock with
a fossilized leaf

Where did the forest treasures come from?

1

2

3

4

5

6

7

8

9

10

11

12

Look for the answers at the end of the book.

A walk in the country
will do us some good!

button

beetle

dog tag

cricket casing
(its old body)

clover

ground cherry

Little Countryside Treasures

a wing nut

a star-shaped
button

a ground cherry

a tuft
of raw wool

a thistle flower

pink peony
petals

dandelion fluff

anthracite,
a glittery rock

a cricket's casing
(its old body)

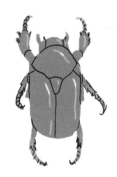

a metallic green
beetle

a dog tag

a four-leaf clover
(what luck!)

Match each treasure to one of the objects on this page.

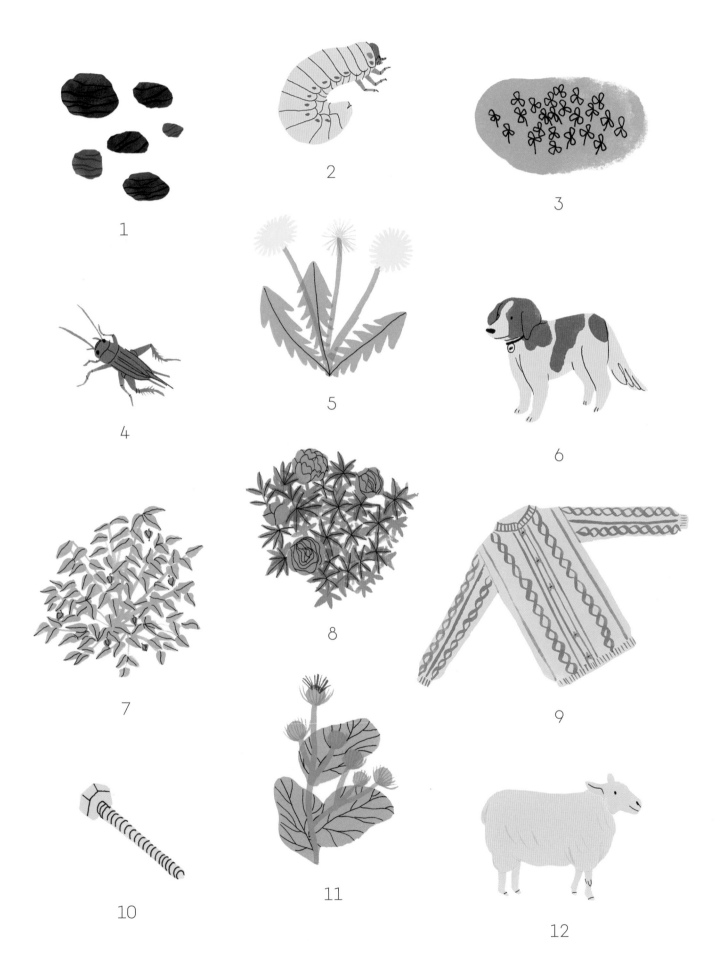

1

2

3

4

5

6

7

8

9

10

11

12

The answers are at the end of the book.

What do you say
to a trip to the park?

feather

action
figure
head

branch

coin

gravel

seeds

Little Park Treasures

a piece of silver
birch bark

a stick-figure
branch

a lock key

milkweed
seeds

an empty
candy wrapper

an action
figure head

a crocus bulb

a metal washer

a duck feather

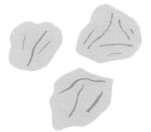

quartz gravel

a coin

a child's ring

Do you see a match for each treasure?

1

2

3

4

5

6

7

8

9

10

11

12

Look for the answers at the end of the book.

It's a perfect day to go to the beach.

boot

bottle

starfish

That's an odd-looking shell you have there.

dinosaur

No, Grandma — it's an urchin skeleton!

cuttlebone

algae

carapace

seashell

mussel

clam

driftwood

Little Beach Treasures

a piece of driftwood

a dried starfish

a doll's boot

an urchin skeleton

a mussel shell

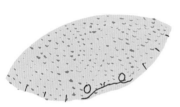

a horseshoe crab carapace

a turret seashell

sea lettuce

a plastic triceratops

a cuttlebone

a bottle with a message inside

an Atlantic Jackknife clam

You know what to do!

1

2

3

5

4

6

8

7

9

10

11

12

Look for the answers at the end of the book.

How do you know about so many treasures, Grandma?!

When I was a little girl, I loved to collect all sorts of things, just like you. Then I'd draw them in a notebook and ask my grandfather to help me identify them.

I want to draw my treasures, too! Could I see your notebook? Do you still have it?

Of course! And while we're looking for it, I'll tell you about the other treasures I've seen on our walks — maybe you noticed them ...

Little (and Big) Living Treasures

weasel

vole

mallard duck

cat

deer

tawny owl

grass snake

swan

squirrel

seagull

frog

otter

heron

dog

kingfisher

partridge

gannet

pigeon

raven

raccoon

toad

crab

falcon

hare

fawn

puffin

rabbit

goose

butterfly

sheep

gull

chicken

chipmunk

cow

beetle

mole

trout

Little Riverside Treasures

1. The fishing lure is tied onto the end of the fishing line to attract fish.

2. The cattail is the reed's fruit. It is made up of seeds.

3. Ceramic is baked clay. It is used to make dishware and other objects.

4. Reusable glass bottles are resealed with metal caps.

5. Crayfish are small, clawed crustaceans that live in freshwater.

6. A chain is made up of links.

7. Pussy willows grow on weeping willow branches. Later, they become flowers.

8. Dragonflies are insects. They have two pairs of delicate, transparent wings.

9. Tufts adorn the tops of reeds.

10. A pebble is a rock fragment. Carried along by the water, it becomes smooth as it tumbles against other rocks and pebbles.

11. Like pebbles, pieces of glass are polished or smoothed as they tumble in rivers or lakes (beach glass) or oceans (sea glass).

12. Snails wear shells, unlike slugs, which don't.

Little City Treasures

1. Square head nails were used in building until the 20th century.

2. A walnut is the fruit of the walnut tree. It grows inside a hard shell.

3. Sunglasses lenses are tinted to dim sunlight's brightness.

4. A dog whistle makes sound only dogs and cats can hear.

5. Decorative stones are often used in flowerbeds.

6. The shape of the gingko leaf is unusual. The gingko tree is from Asia.

7. Marbles are traditionally made of glass. Many have different-colored streaks inside.

8. Necklaces are a type of jewelry often made with strung beads.

9. Barrettes help keep your hair in place — and out of your eyes!

10. When magnolia flower petals fall off, they are replaced by leaves.

11. A pick, or plectrum, is used to strum the guitar strings to make sound.

12. Wooden matches are kept in little boxes to keep them dry.

Little Forest Treasures

1. To open a soda can, you lift the small tab on its top.

2. A maple tree's fruit is called a key, or samara. It is shaped like a wing.

3. Tucked inside a prickly casing, the chestnut is the fruit of the chestnut tree.

4. The goldfinch is a small yellow perching bird that lays blue eggs.

5. As snakes grow, they molt, or shed, leaving their too-small skins behind.

6. Pinecones are the fruit of the pine tree. They open in dry weather.

7. Acorns are the fruit of the oak tree. Their little caps are called cupules.

8. Young fern shoots, or fiddleheads, can be eaten. Yum!

9. Bell-shaped lily of the valley flowers grow in clusters.

10. A fossil is the trace of plant or animal matter that has been preserved in rock.

11. Partridges are non-migratory birds that spend most of their lives on the ground. They live in small groups.

12. Holly is a bush that produces small, bright red berries.

Little Countryside Treasures

1. Anthracite is a glittery black rock that is partly made up of carbon. It can be used for fuel.

2. Before becoming an adult insect, a beetle begins life as a larva.

3. Clover is a three-leafed, and sometimes four-leafed, plant.

4. To grow, crickets shed their too-small casings; what's left behind is called a molt.

5. Dandelion fluff is the plant's seeds. Blow on it and watch them fly!

6. Dog tags identify a dog's name and owner.

7. Ground cherries are small, husk-covered berries. When they are ripe, they fall from the plant.

8. Peony flowers' silky petals can be many different colors.

9. You might find a star-shaped button on a shirt or sweater.

10. A wing nut is part of a nut-and-screw duo. These fasteners hold things together.

11. Thistles have rounded flowers with tiny, hook-like barbs that stick to people's clothes and animals' fur.

12. Before it's washed, carded and spun, raw wool looks like stuffing.

Little Park Treasures

1. Action figures sometimes have removable heads.

2. Metal washers help support tightened screws and bolts.

3. Silver birch bark is smooth and paper-like.

4. White quartz gravel is often used in gardens and parks.

5. Some ring bands are adjustable.

6. This candy wrapper belongs in the garbage!

7. Crocus plants grow from bulbs.

8. Male mallard ducks have colorful feathers.

9. Change purses hold coins.

10. Some locks open with keys.

11. Little twigs can be tied together to make stick figures.

12. When a milkweed seed pod ripens, it opens, and the seeds are carried on the wind.

Little Beach Treasures

1. The little plastic boot belongs to this doll.

2. A mussel is a mollusk, a creature with a soft body and hard shell.

3. Driftwood is wood that fell in the water or broke off shipwrecks.

4. Animals that eat horseshoe crabs sometimes leave the carapaces behind.

5. Long, cone-shaped turret shells are home to small sea snails.

6. This little plastic triceratops is a toy someone left behind.

7. Sea lettuce is green algae that grows in shallow water.

8. Starfish shrink as they dry out.

9. When sea urchins die, their spines fall out. Their skeletons sometimes wash up on the beach.

10. Cuttlefish are soft-bodied creatures with a hard interior shell, or bone.

11. Atlantic Jackknife clams are mollusks, soft-bodied creatures with hard shells, that hide in the sand.

12. Messages — or treasure maps! — can be tucked inside bottles and left for others to find.